Zimmerman Academy:
The New Normal

by

Kathi Daley

Books by Kathi Daley

Come for the murder, stay for the romance.

Zoe Donovan Cozy Mystery:

Halloween Hijinks
The Trouble With Turkeys
Christmas Crazy
Cupid's Curse
Big Bunny Bump-off
Beach Blanket Barbie
Maui Madness
Derby Divas
Haunted Hamlet
Turkeys, Tuxes, and Tabbies
Christmas Cozy
Alaskan Alliance
Matrimony Meltdown
Soul Surrender
Heavenly Honeymoon
Hopscotch Homicide
Ghostly Graveyard
Santa Sleuth
Shamrock Shenanigans

Zimmerman Academy Shorts:

The New Normal

Paradise Lake Cozy Mystery:
Pumpkins in Paradise
Snowmen in Paradise
Bikinis in Paradise
Christmas in Paradise
Puppies in Paradise
Halloween in Paradise

Whales and Tails Cozy Mystery:
Romeow and Juliet
The Mad Catter
Grimm's Furry Tail
Much Ado About Felines
Legend of Tabby Hollow
Cat of Christmas Past
A Tale of Two Tabbies – *February 2016*

Seacliff High Mystery:
The Secret
The Curse
The Relic
The Conspiracy
The Grudge

Road to Christmas Romance:
Road to Christmas Past

Note from the author: *Zimmerman Academy: The New Normal* is the first in a new series of novellas that will be told from the point of view of some of the minor characters from the Zoe Donovan Cozy Mystery Series. This first story is told from Zoe's best friend Ellie's point of view. It takes place over the same four-day period that *Shamrock Shenanigans*, Zoe Donovan Mystery Book 19, takes place. Ellie receives some bad news, meets a new man, and helps to solve a murder while Zak and Zoe are out of the country.

Chapter 1

Thursday, February 11

Have you ever had one of those moments where all the little heartbreaks you've been bravely telling yourself aren't that big a deal come crashing down in one huge tidal wave of emotion, demanding that you *finally* acknowledge how you actually feel?

"Ms. Davis, do you understand what I am saying?" Dr. Carter asked from his seat across the desk.

I looked at the doctor. My eyes filled with tears that had been waiting for months to be shed. I nodded my head as I let the reality of the situation sink in.

"Modern medicine is an evolving science. What is impossible today may very well be possible tomorrow. You are young. You have time. Maybe in a year or two I will be able to give you a different answer."

I wiped the tears from my face with the back of my hand. "Thank you," I said in a small voice that was barely more than a whisper. I stood up, gathered my things, and hurried from the office. Somehow I managed to make it to my car before I completely broke down and let all the pain, disappointment, sorrow, and grief I'd been holding at bay gush forth in one huge mental meltdown.

I wrapped my arms around my waist and leaned my head against the steering wheel of my car. I sobbed for everything I had lost, the baby I would never hold, and the emptiness that was left when everything else had been stripped away. I felt so totally hopeless and alone.

My downward spiral began just before Christmas, when Ellie's Beach Hut, the restaurant I'd spent almost two years building from the ground up, burned to the ground, almost killing my best friend, Zoe Donovan, in the process. The Beach Hut was my first venture on my own as an adult and I'd put a lot into it physically, financially, and emotionally. I can't convey the hollowness I felt when I viewed the product of those years reduced to nothing more than a pile of ashes.

Losing my business, however, wasn't the worst thing that happened to me that day. Losing Levi was so much harder. Levi Denton had been my best friend along with Zoe since we were in kindergarten and our teacher had sat us at tables of three by last name. The three of us became a best friend trio and were pretty much inseparable from that point forward. Two years ago my feelings for Levi became a bit more personal, and one year ago we officially became boyfriend and girlfriend. I love Levi. I will always love Levi. But the reality is that we want different things in life. The most important thing to me is having children of my own, while Levi has been quite upfront about the fact that children are nowhere on his radar.

We decided to spilt this past Christmas. We both knew it was the right thing to do to preserve our friendship. I knew it would be hard and there would be a period of adjustment, but what tore at my soul more than anything was the fact that Levi had moved on so easily, while my heart still grieved for what could have been, every minute of every day.

And then today, when Dr. Carter informed me that I wasn't a candidate for the operation I hoped would allow me to have the children my heart longed for, I saw that everything good and normal in my life was suddenly gone, and all that remained was an empty future filled with darkness and despair.

I really wanted to call Zoe and pour out my sorrow, but she was in Ireland with her husband, Zak, on a murder mystery weekend. I wasn't completely sure what the time difference was, but I was pretty sure it was the middle of the night there.

I realized I really did need to pull myself together so I dug through my purse for a tissue. Pulling down my visor, I glanced into the attached mirror.

Yikes.

I was supposed to pick up the new math teacher for Zimmerman Academy in two hours. It was more than an hour's drive to the airport and I knew I wouldn't have time to go home before heading there, so I used the little bit of makeup I had in my purse to try to repair the damage my river of tears had created.

Zimmerman Academy was born when Zak and Zoe began to consider the lives they'd lead once they had children of their own. Zak is some sort of a genius, and Zoe is intuitive and clever herself, so there's a good chance their offspring will be exceptional. The problem is that all Ashton Falls has to offer in terms of educational opportunities is average. Neither Zoe nor Zak has any desire to move to a town where an exceptional education can be found, so they decided to bring an exceptional education to them by building their own private school for gifted children. While they don't have any children of their own yet, they do have three minors living with them, and it appears they have grown into a family as real as any you're likely to find.

After the Beach Hut burned down, Zak offered me a job running the kitchen at the Academy. Currently, the school is housed in a building without a kitchen, but the new facility is due to open next fall and will have a full kitchen for both the day students and the boarders.

In the meantime, I help out where I can, and today the way I was helping out was by driving to Bryton Lake to pick up the new math teacher and his family. Zak has rented them a nice house at the edge of town, and I'd promised to help the newest residents of the small alpine hamlet we call home get settled in.

Once I repaired my makeup to the best of my ability, I started my car and pulled out of the parking lot of the medical facility. The drive from Ashton Falls to Bryton Lake was a beautiful one that I usually enjoyed, but we'd received quite a bit of fresh snow over the past few days and the roads were icy. I just hoped the stormy weather across the nation wouldn't cause the flight to be delayed. The last thing I wanted to do was spend the day sitting in the airport with nothing more for company than depressing thoughts about my empty life.

Six hours later I glanced at the flight board and groaned. As it turned out, the flight *was* late. Four hours late. Pretty much every single flight into or out of our small airport had been canceled or delayed. I paced back and forth mentally cursing the weather, the airline, and the man whose imminent arrival had caused me to be at the airport in the first place. I realize my silent rant was counterproductive, but after the day I'd had, I felt I deserved to wallow in self-pity and outrage.

People who know me would say I'm usually pretty even-tempered. Zoe is the emotional firecracker in the best friend trio, Levi is the wild and untamed one, and I'm the stable, calm, and steady one. I've tried to maintain a positive attitude in spite of everything that has happened, but finding out that I am not eligible for the surgery that would allow me to have children had drained what was left of my self-control, and Brady Matthews's tardiness was threatening to destroy my last shred of patience.

"Ms. Davis?"

I stopped pacing and turned around to see a man with the bluest eyes I had ever seen struggling to juggle a backpack, a large diaper bag, a toddler in each arm, and a little girl who looked to be about four holding onto his belt loop.

"Brady Matthews?"

"Yes, and this is Hudson and Haden," he nodded toward the toddlers in his arms, "and Holly," he looked at the girl as his side.

"Here, let me help you." Suddenly my irritation turned to compassion. The poor man looked exhausted. Here I was, whining to myself about having to wait in an airport for four hours. I never once stopped to think about how exhausting it must be to be stuck on an airplane for hours with three small children.

"Thanks." Brady handed me one of the twins, I think Haden, who stuck his hand in his mouth but didn't scream when I took him in my arms.

"I assume you have luggage?"

"A few bags. I'm having most of our stuff shipped. It should be here in a few days. In the meantime, I brought what I thought we'd need to get by."

"How about I get us a cart?" I offered. "We can load up all the luggage and take it to the front. I'll run and get the car while you wait with the luggage and the children so we don't have to haul everything through the snow to the parking lot."

Brady smiled. A perfectly wonderful smile that made his eyes crinkle in the corners just the tiniest bit. "Thanks. That sounds like a good plan. Is there a restaurant in the airport? I'm afraid the kids haven't eaten anything other than the snacks I brought along since this morning."

"There's a restaurant, but it's terrible. I know of a great little café not far from here. We can stop there if you'd like."

"Sounds perfect."

It took longer than I'd predicted to retrieve Brady's luggage, get the car, pick everyone up, and get to the café. Traveling with three children who all needed to be buckled into car seats was quite the production. Luckily, Zak had thought to strap the car seats we'd purchased into my car before he left for Ireland, because to be honest, with everything that had been going through my mind of late, I'm not sure I would have remembered.

Once we'd settled into the booth at the café and ordered, all three kids lay down on the bench between Brady and me and fell asleep. Brady thought it would be best to let them nap until the food arrived. It had, after all, been a *very* long day.

I asked Brady about his trip as a way to break the ice.

"To be honest I've had better. The four of us had to wake up at five o'clock this morning in order to make it to the airport on time, only to find out that our flight was delayed. When it did finally arrive, I found out that there was a problem with the tickets and all they had available were four middle seats scattered throughout the plane. Fortunately, a family of four who did have assignments together gave us their seats because their children were teenagers and would be fine on their own."

"Sounds awful."

"It got worse. Because our plane was late taking off, it was also late arriving, and we missed our connecting flight. I was on the verge of breaking down into very unmanly tears when I was told all the flights for the remainder of the day were full so we'd have to wait on standby and hope something opened up."

"They wanted you to wait indefinitely in an airport with three children?"

He nodded. "We were lucky. Four angels in the form of teenagers on their way to a concert took pity on us and gave up their seats."

"That sort of renews your faith in humanity."

"It really does. I don't know what I would have done if it hadn't been for the kindness of strangers today."

I smiled.

"I can't wait to get settled into our new home. The kids have had a rough year and a half and it will be good to get them stabilized. I'm hoping that for the first time since the twins were born we'll be able to settle into some sort of a normal routine."

I looked at the twins, who couldn't be more than eighteen months old. "Zak said you're a widower?"

The light faded from Brady's eyes. I supposed it probably was too soon to ask and regretted doing it immediately.

"It's been fourteen months now."

I waited quietly for him to elaborate if he chose to do so but didn't push. Somehow, though, I had the feeling he wanted to share his struggle with someone who would listen and offer support.

"Trish had a tough time when she was pregnant with the boys. She suffered high blood pressure and other complications associated with preeclampsia. She wanted the boys to have a fighting chance, so she insisted on continuing the pregnancy even when her own life was at risk. After she delivered we hoped she'd bounce back, but she never really did. She was weak and her immune system suffered. She developed pneumonia when the boys were four months old. She died a few days later."

"I'm so sorry."

"It was such a dark time in my life. In all our lives. I had a hard time accepting what had happened, so the kids went to live with my parents. I missed them, but I knew I couldn't be there for them physically or emotionally. Their staying with my parents seemed to be the best solution. Eventually I moved in with them as well. At the time it seemed easier than getting on with my own life. In the long run it wasn't."

I placed my hand over Brady's. He looked into my eyes. "I don't know why I'm telling you all this."

"I'm a good listener and I understand how it is to have your entire life turned upside down. While I haven't suffered anything as devastating and life-altering as losing a spouse and being left alone to raise three children, I've had a series of life-altering events occur over the past few months, and to be honest, most days I feel like I'm wandering aimlessly in a world that no longer makes sense."

"That's exactly how I felt at first. It was like every day existed in isolation and nothing fit together. I can remember longing for the comfort of everyday routines. Waking to Trish's smile. Making coffee while she saw to the kids. Reading the paper together, me the funnies and her the business section."

"I like the funnies." I smiled. "I always read them first. I think curling up with the funnies page is the main reason I've never given up my old-fashioned paper-and-ink subscription."

"It's not the same reading them online," Brady agreed.

"I totally understand what you're saying about a normal routine, though. My boyfriend and I decided to end things a few months ago. We're still friends—best friends—but we wanted different things out of life. I knew there would be an adjustment period, but what I didn't count on was the feeling of emptiness that washes over me when I realize he won't be joining me for dinner and we won't be watching our favorite television show together. I actually cried the other day when I noticed how lonely my toothbrush looked in the holder we'd bought last summer."

"I left Trish's toothbrush in the holder next to mine until I moved in with my parents."

It felt good to have someone who *really* understood how displaced I'd been feeling. Zoe had tried to be there for me, but I could see a look of confusion in her eyes when I told her about things like missing Levi's toothbrush and how *Survivor* just wasn't fun to watch alone.

We paused our conversation when the waitress brought the food. We decided that if the kids woke up on their own they could eat now, but if they didn't we'd box up their meals and bring them with us. The poor little things looked like they were out for the count.

After the waitress left we veered onto general topics of conversation such as the weather, the Academy, and the quirky yet totally lovable people who called Ashton Falls home. The snow had begun to come down harder, so we ate quickly, ordered to-go boxes for the kids' food, and started the long, slow trek up the mountain. By the time I pulled up in front of the house Zak had rented for the family I was almost cross-eyed from trying to follow the narrow, winding road that was covered with snow.

"How about I go in and turn on lights and open doors before we begin unloading everyone?" I offered. "I told the contractors who were here this morning to leave the lights and the heat on, but it's obvious they shut the lights. I only hope they left the heat on. Otherwise it's going to be cold inside."

"Okay," Brady answered. "I'll begin the process of unbuckling everyone."

I trudged up to the front door through the knee-deep snowdrifts. I was about to fish the key out of my purse when I noticed the front door was cracked open. I slowly pushed the door and stepped inside. Thankfully, the heat, unlike the lights, had been left on. I switched on the overhead lights in the main part of the house and then headed out to help Brady bring everyone inside.

He somehow managed to nestle both Haden and Hudson into his arms and I picked up Holly and followed him up the snowy walk and into the house.

Brady stopped in the middle of the living room and looked around. "Nice."

"I think you'll be comfortable here. The house has four bedrooms, all on the second floor. You can use one for an office or den if you plan to have the twins share."

"It sounds perfect. Let me change the boys' diapers and slip them into their pj's and then I'll get my things out of your car."

"Daddy?" Holly lifted her head from my shoulder. I wondered if she'd wake up when I'd picked her up, but she must be a heavy sleeper because she hadn't stirred until this point.

"Right here, honey."

Holly struggled to get down. I set her on the floor and she ran over to her father. The poor thing seemed to be feeling insecure about the move. Not that I blamed her. The boys were too young to understand what was going on, but for a four-year-old being uprooted and forced to leave everything she had ever known must be terrifying.

"The bedrooms are at the top of the stairs. You'll find two cribs in one of them.

Why don't you get the kids settled and I'll grab the luggage?"

"Are you sure? The large suitcase is pretty heavy."

"I'm sure. I'm stronger than I look."

By the time I unloaded the car and returned to the living area, Brady had all three of his children changed into warm pajamas and snuggled up on the sofa. He'd even managed to start the fire, which had been prepared so that all you had to do was light a match. The twins were drinking bottles, which they held themselves, and Holly was sitting on her dad's lap with a child's cup in her hand. It looked like she'd be asleep within minutes.

"Did you figure out the bedroom situation?" I asked.

"We did. And thank you very much. Holly loved the purple comforter on her bed. Purple is her favorite color."

I smiled. "Mine too."

"Zak leased a car for you. It's in the garage. The keys are on the kitchen table. I brought the car seats in; they're with the luggage in the hall."

"Thank you. I can see I'm going to love working at the Academy. Everyone has been so nice and helpful."

"We're a family. It really is the best place to work. Let's see, the thermostat is on the wall near the entrance to the kitchen and there's food in the refrigerator; not a lot, but enough to make breakfast for your family. There are extra linens and blankets in the closet at the end of the hall on the second story and the TV remote is in the drawer of the little table next to the sofa. I'll be by tomorrow morning to introduce you to the babysitter. Her name is Stephanie. She's really nice and very responsible. I'm sure the kids will love her, but I thought it best she spend some time with them before you start teaching your classes."

"Thanks. I agree it will be easier on Holly especially if she knows the babysitter before she's left alone with her. Do you know when I'm supposed to start classes?"

"Zak will be back from his trip on Monday. I know he plans to meet with you on Tuesday. I guess you can discuss a start date at that time. Until then, I'm here to help in any way I can."

Holly had fallen asleep in Brady's arms. "I'm going to put her to bed. Can you keep an eye on the boys until I get back?"

"Absolutely."

I sat down on the sofa between the two toddlers, who had both finished their bottles and were fast asleep. I scooped

Haden into my arms and settled him onto my chest. It felt so right to be holding a baby. I wrapped his blanket around him and snuggled him next to my heart. What I wouldn't give for one of my own someday.

I looked up to see Brady watching me. He smiled and I smiled back. Brady picked up Hudson and cuddled him into his arms. He sat down next to me and we sat in silence, each lost in our own thoughts yet finding comfort in the toddlers we held.

When I noticed Brady nodding off I suggested we put the boys to bed. After they were tucked in I confirmed a time to bring Stephanie by and then headed out to my car. The solitary ride back to Zoe and Zak's, where I was staying while they were away, seemed so lonely after the warmth and companionship I'd shared with Brady and his children. I loved the little boathouse I lived in, and my dog, Shep, was the best, but my heart yearned for someone special to come home to at the end of each day.

I parked in the back of the house near the kitchen. When I walked in through the side door I noticed the lights were on. The dogs all ran up to greet me, and I let them out into the yard for a quick run before heading into the living room, where I found Levi watching a movie on the giant flat screen television.

"Levi, what are you doing here?"

"I was waiting for Zoe. The door was open."

"Zoe and Zak are in Ireland. You'd know that if you were ever around."

I watched as a sadness came over Levi's face. I know I was being snappy, but somehow, seeing him sitting there just like old times, made me feel sadder than I was already.

"I know I haven't been around much," Levi answered. "I just thought it would be easier if I stayed away for a while."

"Easier for you so you have more time to spend with your new girlfriend?"

"That's not what I mean, and she isn't—or I guess I should say, wasn't—my girlfriend. Exactly."

"What do you mean *wasn't*?"

"I mean she's dead."

"Dead?" Suddenly all my anger melted away. Poor Levi. "What happened?"

"I'm not sure. I wasn't able to get hold of Sheriff Salinger to confirm the details. I do know they found her body in her apartment this morning after she didn't show up for work. I didn't find out until after school let out. I've been trying to call

Zoe ever since, but she isn't picking up. I forgot about the whole Ireland thing."

I crossed the room and wrapped my arms around Levi in an offering of support. He'd been my best friend before he was my ex. Somehow, if I wanted to remain best friends, I needed to get past the *ex* part of our history. "I'm so sorry. I know the two of you were close."

"We were friends. She was a nice person. I want to find out what happened. I hoped Zoe would use her influence with Salinger to get the answers no one seems willing to share."

"Zoe does seem to have a way of gaining cooperation from our grouchy sheriff," I admitted. "But we've helped out in the past as well. He knows that. Maybe if we go talk to him together he'll tell us what he knows."

"You'll go with me?"

"Yes. I have to take the babysitter over to meet the new math teacher for the Academy at around ten. Why don't we hit up Salinger first thing, when he'll most likely be in his office?"

"I have a class at eight, but maybe I can get a sub for first period. A couple of staff members owe me favors."

"Okay. If you can get a sub we'll meet at the sheriff's office at seven thirty. Once we hear what he has to say we can take it from there."

Levi hugged me tight. "Thanks, El." He took a step back and looked me in the eye. "You know I love you."

I smiled. "I know. I love you too."

Chapter 2

Friday, February 12

Levi and I came prepared to bribe Salinger into speaking to us. Levi carried a bag with a dozen gooey doughnuts and I carried an extra tall vanilla latte, just the kind he liked. Luckily, the front door to the main lobby from the street was open, and it was early enough that Salinger was the only one in the office.

"Where's Donovan?" he barked the minute we walked in the front door.

"Ireland," I answered as I handed him the large coffee cup.

"Damn. I was afraid it was something like that. I've left twenty messages and she hasn't returned a one."

"Don't feel bad," I said. "Levi and I have left a ton of messages as well and she hasn't returned ours either. I bet the cell service isn't operating where she's staying for some reason. I tried calling Zak's line, but he didn't pick up either."

Salinger looked at Levi. "I bet those doughnuts you're holding are supposed to soften me up so I'll tell you what I know about Ms. Kramer."

Levi handed the bag to Salinger. "Is it working?"

"No, but I wanted to talk to you anyway. Let's go into my office."

Salinger locked the front door, I imagined because there would be no one in the reception area until the clerk arrived at eight, and led us down the hall to his office. Levi and I sat down while Salinger dug through the bag of doughnuts, looking for his favorites.

"It appears," Salinger began after taking a couple of bites of the sugary treat, "Ms. Kramer ingested a lethal dose of sleeping pills sometime between ten o'clock Wednesday night and two o'clock Thursday morning. The coroner is working on whittling down the time span, but for now that four-hour window is what we have to work with."

"You suspect foul play?" Levi asked. "You don't think it was suicide?"

"Is there a reason Ms. Kramer might have wanted to kill herself?"

Levi hesitated. He glanced at me and then back at Salinger. "Maddie and I fought on Wednesday night. I didn't kill her, but when I left she was pretty upset, and she'd been drinking, but no, I don't think she'd kill herself."

"Do you mind telling me what you fought about?"

"She wanted us to move in together. I told her I wasn't interested in that sort of a relationship and she accused me of using her."

"Did you have a sexual relationship with Ms. Kramer?"

Levi glanced at me, a look of apology in his eyes, before he answered. "Yes. We had a physical relationship. But at no point did I indicate that I was interested in settling down."

I felt my heart explode with pain and betrayal. I'd suspected Levi was sleeping with Maddie, but I didn't know for certain it was true until now. We'd broken up less than two months ago, after a year-long relationship. It hurt that he'd moved on so easily.

"What time did you leave Ms. Kramer's apartment?"

"Around nine."

"Did she say anything to you that would indicate that she was expecting anyone to come by?"

"No."

"Did she seem overly distraught?"

"She was upset, but like I said, Maddie didn't seem the type to end her own life. She had too much self-esteem for that."

"Could she have accidentally overdosed?"

Levi didn't answer right away.

"Did you find an empty pill bottle?" I asked.

Salinger turned his attention to me. "No, we didn't."

"If Maddie was alone and she either accidentally overdosed or intentionally committed suicide, the empty pill bottle would be nearby. I doubt she'd bother to remove the bottle from the immediate area if she was intending to kill herself; likewise, if she simply intended to use the pills to induce sleep, she would have no reason to discard the bottle. If the bottle wasn't in the apartment, there's a good chance another party removed it. The only reason I can see to do that is to cover up a murder."

"Good point."

"Maddie lived in an apartment building. Chances are someone saw something. If I were you, I'd take a look around to see if the pill bottle rolled under the sofa or behind a chair. If you don't find it, I'd start looking for suspects."

"You filling in for Donovan while she's away?" Salinger teased.

"Yes," I answered quite seriously, "I guess I am."

"I need to get to work," Levi informed Salinger. "I have a class in twenty minutes. Will you please let me know what you find out? I didn't love Mattie and I didn't see us having a long-term relationship, but I did like her, and I cared about her. If she was murdered, I want to see her killer caught."

"The two of you have helped Donovan investigate enough times that I suppose some of her natural ability could have rubbed off on you. While you aren't my first choices I'm shorthanded. If you want to stop back this afternoon we can chat again."

"Thanks. I appreciate that." Levi stood up.

"When will Donovan be back?" Salinger asked me.

"Monday."

"All right. If you get hold of her tell her to call me."

Levi and I let ourselves out of the office. The clerk had arrived while we were chatting with Salinger so the door had been unlocked.

"Do you have time to meet up later this afternoon?" Levi asked.

I wanted to say no. I wanted to remind the man I'd loved for what seemed like forever that he'd hurt me deeply and I needed time to heal. But I didn't. I told him I'd be happy to meet with him as long as Zoe's parents were able to keep Alex and Scooter at their place for one more night. I was supposed to be child sitting, but I'd asked them to watch the kids while I went to Bryton Lake to pick up Brady. When it had gotten so late I'd called and arranged for them to spend the night.

We arranged to meet at three thirty, after Levi finished his classes for the day. I didn't need to tell him how much he'd hurt me by jumping into Maddie's bed before ours had even grown cold. I could tell by the way he was avoiding eye contact that he knew exactly how I felt.

Decompressing Levi and his motivation for doing what he'd done was going to get me nowhere, so I decided to focus on my morning with Brady. I'd take Stephanie over to meet the kids, and if they all seemed comfortable together, maybe he and I would run a few errands so they could spend some time together as sort of a trial run for when he'd need to leave them for a full day while he was at work.

I very much wanted to be Brady's friend. There was something about him that I was immediately drawn to. Maybe it was the fact that we were both struggling with finding a sense of normalcy, but I felt like he understood me better than anyone else right then.

"Picking out the right diaper is tricky," Brady informed me after we'd settled the kids with Stephanie and headed to the store. "This one," he picked up a box with a blue lid, "fits the best. The sizing is far superior to say this one." He pointed to the box with a red lid.

"So get the one with the blue lid."

"The thing is, the ones in the red lid are much more absorbent than the other ones. I'd estimate that the diapers in the blue lid need to be changed twenty percent more often than those in the red lid."

"Is changing more often a problem?"

"Not during the day. I like to keep the boys fresh and dry, and the diapers in the blue lid are less expensive, so even though I use more it works out to about the same cost. The problem comes into play at night. I've found that if they're wearing the more absorbent diapers they tend to sleep longer."

"So get both. Use the better-fitting diapers during the day. That's when they'll be moving around and fit will be more important. Use the more absorbent diapers at night."

"The perfect solution. You're going to knock this parenting thing out of the park when you have children of your own. It took me a year to figure out the trick of buying both rather than choosing just one brand."

I tried not to let my smile slip, but it must have.

"Sensitive subject?"

"A little. Maybe I'll tell you about it sometime. For now, let's try to figure out which brand of toddler food to buy."

"That's where it gets really tricky. I've developed a spreadsheet to help me determine the best products based on taste, nutrition, and price."

"You're kidding."

"'Fraid not. Once we get the toddler food I say we move on to cat supplies. I'm afraid I don't have any research to back up my purchases in that department."

"I can't believe there was a cat sleeping in Holly's bed when you went in to check on her last night. I guess she got in at some point during the day. The front door was cracked open when we got there last night."

"I spoke to the very nice woman who lives next door and she told me the cat belonged to the former owners. I gather they just left her when they moved. She's been feeding her, but she assured me that if I was willing to adopt her that would be a much better solution."

"And you're okay with Holly having a cat?"

Brady nodded. "She's been taking this move hard. She misses her grandparents. I think the cat will be good for her."

I had to agree. Holly had been quiet and sullen the previous day, but when Stephanie and I arrived this morning she couldn't wait to introduce us to Mittens, who seemed to be a perfect pet for the young girl. Mittens was a small female cat with long gray fur and four white paws. She really was precious and she seemed to adore Holly.

"Is there a farmers market in town?" Brady asked.

"Only during the summer. During the winter you're pretty much limited to what the grocer stocks, but most of the time the produce is fresh. I'd avoid fruits and veggies that are out of season, though. The flavor really isn't there."

I watched Brady's hands as he picked out three large tomatoes. He held the tomatoes the way he held his twins, with a gentle strength. I really shouldn't be noticing the hands of a man so newly widowed, but I found that I was having the best day. Not only had Holly been cheerful and talkative when I arrived that morning but the twins had toddled over to me as soon as I walked in and reached up their arms to be picked up. Picking them both up at the same time without dropping either was hard, but I managed just fine and was rewarded by sloppy kisses that melted my heart.

"So, where do you stand on pasta?" Brady asked.

"Pasta?"

"Most of the women I know won't touch the stuff. Too many carbs."

"I love pasta."

"Me too." Brady tossed three different varieties into the basket before filling me in on the history of the starchy stuff.

In spite of the running monologue—and the fact that I learned more about the science of shopping than I'd ever really wanted to—I had a really good time with Brady. I could see why Zak and Brady had hit it off right away. Zak was a billionaire and still had every item he purchased reduced to a variable based on price, quality, and a bunch of other things I didn't understand. Zoe had given up trying to keep up with Zak's logic long ago and simply let him take care of all the shopping.

After we took the groceries back to Brady's place, I took Stephanie home while Brady made lunch for all of us. I had to meet Levi at three thirty, but there was no way I was going to turn down the chance to get to know Holly, Haden, and Hudson a little better. There was nothing like a smile from a child to ease even the most intense heartache.

After lunch Brady put the kids down for a nap while I started in on the dishes. I was just finishing up when my phone rang.

"Hey, Salinger. What's up?"

"I wanted to let you know that you were right. We searched the entire apartment and didn't find a pill bottle. I had the ME's office test the residue in her wineglass and there was evidence that the sleeping pills were ground up and added to the wine. I have to head out now; there's a pileup on the highway. But I'm going to need to speak to Levi again. I know he's in class right now, so I called you. Not only did we find pill residue in Ms. Kramer's wineglass but we found a second wineglass in the sink. Levi's prints are all over it."

My heart sank. "You know he wouldn't…"

"I know. That's the only reason I didn't drag him out of class. Just let him know I'm going to need to have another conversation with him when I get back into town. It could be several hours."

"Okay, I'll tell him. And thanks for giving him the benefit of the doubt."

"Boy's still gonna need an alibi."

"Yeah. I know. I'll ask him about it."

I took a deep breath and let it out slowly after I hung up.

"Bad news?" Brady asked from the doorway behind me.

"A local woman—a teacher at the high school—died. They think she was murdered."

"That's horrible. I'm so sorry. Were you close?"

"No. Not at all. Still, someone I am close to was good friends with her. I'm afraid the fact that he was at her place shortly before she died is going to complicate things."

Brady frowned. "You don't think your friend…?"

"No," I said with conviction. "Levi wouldn't hurt a fly. Luckily, Sheriff Salinger seems to know that as well."

"That was the sheriff on the phone?"

"Yeah. We were supposed to meet later, but there was an accident on the highway coming into town."

Brady looked confused. "Are you some sort of a private investigator?"

I laughed. "Hardly. That's Zoe's gig. I have on occasion helped her investigate some deaths, and because Levi was a friend of Maddie Kramer's, I guess I feel a certain investment in seeing how the investigation turns out. Unlike Zoe, however, I have no intention of playing the hero and leaping into the fray. I'll help out of I can, but I plan to remain fray adjacent."

Brady looked at me like I was crazy. Who could blame him? It was unusual for a sheriff to consult with the locals about ongoing investigations.

"I was thinking that the kids and I might like to tour the town tomorrow. If you aren't busy maybe you'd like to come with us. I'll even buy you lunch."

"I'd love to. What time were you thinking?"

"Maybe around ten?"

"I'll pick you up. It'll be easier if I drive because I know where everything is. Dress warmly. We'll want to park and walk around the shops on Main Street. There are a couple of good places to eat on Main as well."

"Sounds like a date."

I had to admit I liked the sound of that.

Levi and I decided to meet at Zak and Zoe's because I was staying there while they were out of town. We took my dog, Shep, Levi's dog, Karloff, Zak's dog, Bella, and Scooter's dog, Digger, for a walk along the lakeshore. Zoe had taken her dog, Charlie, with her to Ireland. Zoe never went anywhere without Charlie. It was odd to realize that Charlie had traveled a lot more broadly than I most likely ever would.

Walking the dogs with Levi along the same path he and I had walked them thousands of times over the years was oddly comforting. This participation in a familiar activity provided a feeling of normalcy to my life at a time when nothing felt normal. I wasn't happy Maddie was dead, but I was glad Levi and I were somewhat forced into a situation that would require us to work together, just like we had in the past.

"I can't imagine who would kill Maddie," Levi said after I explained about the ground-up pills in the wine.

"We'll figure it out. We always do. I know Zoe isn't here, but she'll be back Monday. I'm sure if we haven't figured it out by then she'll pitch in and help. Let's not mention it to her if we get through to her, though. She'll only worry, and there isn't anything she can do from Ireland. I think it's best to let her have her vacation without having to spend all her time thinking about murder for once."

"Agreed. Although I'm sure Salinger told her what was going on. He did say he left a bunch of messages."

"When I got home I realized he left the messages on the house phone. I'm not sure he even has Zoe's new cell number."

"Okay, so if we're investigating this on our own where do we start?"

"By figuring out exactly what you're going to tell Salinger when he gets back."

Levi didn't answer right away, He picked up a stick and tossed it down the beach. All the dogs took off chasing it.

"Something on your mind?" I asked.

"I'm just afraid that talking about this is going to be weird for you. I'm enjoying our walk. It feels like old times. I hate to ruin the moment."

While I agreed with him, Salinger was going to want answers. Our time would be well spent coming up with some.

"I know our decision to return to best friend status was mutual. And I don't regret the decision we made. I think in the long run it will prove to be the right one. But it's been hard. Harder than I imagined it would be. It really hurt that you moved on so quickly. The fact that you did made me feel that what we had hadn't meant as much to you as it meant to me."

Levi stopped walking. He turned and looked at me. "I'm sorry I hurt you. That was the last thing I wanted to do. My relationship with Maddie meant nothing to me. We simply got along well and had a few good times. I don't know why I slept with her. I guess it made me hurt a little less. At least for a while. Maddie never had even a tiny piece of my heart. Not the way you do. I love you and I love Zoe. You're the most important people in my life and I would never want to hurt either of you."

I couldn't prevent the tear that slipped down my cheek. "I know. I love you too. It doesn't change anything and I know we're best as friends. It might have taken me a little longer, but I feel like I might finally be ready to move on. I know if I can it won't hurt so much to see you with someone else."

Levi took my hand. We walked along in silence until we hit the end of the beach. We turned around and started back. I was glad we'd had this talk. It had been long overdue. In a way I felt like my shattered heart had been at least partially repaired as, for the first time in a long time, I found myself looking forward to what lay ahead rather than backward at what I'd lost.

Chapter 3

Salinger wanted to talk to Levi alone, so I sat in the lobby of the sheriff's station, driving myself crazy as I imagined every horrible outcome to the situation. There was no part of me that thought Levi was guilty, but there was a small one that believed Salinger would arrest him if he didn't have an alibi. Which he didn't. We never had gotten around to coming up with a strategy, but Levi had confided that after he left Maddie's that night he went home, watched a movie, and then went to bed.

He said no one had seen him, and he hadn't answered the phone or talked to anyone. There was absolutely no way for him to prove to anyone where he was or what he was doing when Maddie was killed.

I was seriously about to jump out of my skin when Brady called, saving me from the embarrassing outburst I was trying to avoid.

"Hey, Brady; what's up?"

"How do you feel about Chinese?"

"The language, the people, or the food?"

"The food. The kids and I are ordering in. We thought you might want to join us."

I looked at Salinger's closed door. As much as Chinese with Brady and the kids sounded like a slice of heaven, I had already promised Levi we would strategize.

"As absolutely perfect as that sounds, I promised to help out a friend tonight. I'm looking forward to tomorrow, though."

"As am I. Now for the next embarrassing question: Do you know where we can get take-out Chinese? If you had agreed to come to dinner I would've just asked you to choose your favorite restaurant, thereby preventing me from having to admit the motivation behind the invite."

I laughed. "Chan's. I have the number in my phone. Hang on." I looked it up and read it to him. "You know, you can just ask if you have questions. You don't need to invite me to dinner just so I'll share my favorite place for takeout."

"I lied. Having you choose the restaurant wasn't really my main motivation. The kids and I wanted to spend some more time with you."

"Then why didn't you just say so?"

I waited for Brady to respond. When he did it was with a tone of uncertainty. "I don't know. It's been a very long time since I've asked a girl to dinner, takeout or otherwise."

Was he asking me out on a date? Naw. He didn't know anyone in town. He probably just wanted someone to talk to.

I watched as Salinger's door opened and Levi walked out with the sheriff behind him. "My friend is here. I have to go. I'll see you tomorrow."

I hung up quickly. I don't know why I didn't want Levi to know I was talking to a man. Brady and I were just friends. I had nothing to hide. Heck, I was a single woman. I had nothing to hide even if we were more than friends. It was a lot harder to make the transition back to just friends with Levi than I'd hoped it would be.

"So?" I asked Levi after we'd said good-bye to Salinger and exited the building.

Levi shrugged. "I was honest. I told him I didn't have an alibi, but I also reiterated that I would never kill Maddie, or anyone else for that matter. It seemed like he believed me. He let me go."

"Did he say whether he had any leads?"

"He didn't say, but I had the feeling he didn't."

"Do you have any idea who might have done it?"

Levi opened my car door for me. "Maybe. I'm not sure. How about we pick up some takeout and go back to your place? We can make a list of possible suspects and motives."

"I'm staying at Zoe's," I reminded him.

"Okay, then let's meet up at Zoe's. I'll pick up the food. Chinese okay?"

I was the first to arrive at the house, so I took the dogs out for a quick run, opened a bottle of Zak's expensive wine, started a fire, and put on some music. Then I decided I'd created much too romantic a scene, so I turned off the music and changed into the rattiest sweats I had with me. The fire was already crackling away and I really wanted the wine, so my countermeasures would have to do.

Levi didn't seem to notice what I was wearing one way or another. He grabbed a pen and a pad of paper, filled a plate with a selection of the pint containers he'd brought, and headed toward the dining table.

"So where do we start?" I asked.

"I'm thinking with a list of suspects. When I was talking to Salinger three names came to mind. They're pretty weak as leads, but at this point they're all we have."

"Okay," I said as I filled my own plate and then sat down across from Levi. "What do you have?"

"Before Maddie and I began," Levi hesitated, "spending time together, she was involved with George Wildwood."

I knew George, who was a math teacher at the high school. He was a slight and nerdy sort of guy. He didn't seem to me to be the type to murder someone, but I didn't know him all that well. "Why would George Wildwood kill Maddie?"

"She told me he was a lot more serious about their relationship than she was. He even gave her the money she needed to pay off some debts."

"Hold on," I interrupted. "George gave Maddie money and then she turned around and started..." I paused this time. We both knew what we were trying not to say. "Spending time with you?"

"Yeah. George was pretty mad. At both of us, but mainly at her. He told me that she led him to believe they were all but engaged."

"Maybe it was a scam."

Levi frowned. "I doubt that. I'm sure George just misread the signals. It happens."

"Why would Maddie take money from him if she wasn't as serious about him as he was about her?"

"They were going to repossess her car. She was desperate, and I guess she used bad judgment."

It sounded to me like Maddie had used her looks to scam poor George, who was socially awkward, out of the money she needed to pay off her debts. Sounded like a good motive to me and I said so. "Okay, who else?"

Levi looked at me. "Maybe this is a bad idea."

"Why? You want to find the killer, don't you?"

"Yeah, it's just that..."

Suddenly I knew. "Your second suspect is someone else you were sleeping with!"

Levi grimaced.

"Even before you were sleeping with Maddie." I shook my head. "Who was it?"

"Beverly Hallmark."

Oh, God. It was even worse than I'd thought. Beverly was a waitress at Lucky's Bar who had been flirting with Levi for a year. The entire time we were dating she'd been coming on to him and taking little jabs at me, the mousey girlfriend.

"How could you sleep with Beverly after all the times she was rude and mean to me?"

Levi didn't answer. Suddenly I found that I agreed with Levi. This wasn't a good idea. I wanted to throw a lamp at him. I could just imagine Beverly's smug face when she managed to do exactly what she had been threatening to do all those months.

"Who else?" I demanded.

"El, you have to understand..."

"Who else?"

"I didn't sleep with anyone else, but I think Maddie's sister could be a suspect. I think her name is Lisa. Maddie told me that she was coming to town to discuss their mother's will. Maddie, being the oldest, was named executor, and it seemed she planned to sell the house Lisa is currently living in."

"I thought you said this woman was nice."

"She was. To me."

Suddenly I wondered what I was doing there. Sweet Brady and his three adorable children were eating Chinese food alone while I was eating with my idiot of an ex.

"She sounds like a horrible person. Maybe we should stop wasting our time trying to find her killer. Sounds like whoever did it was justified."

"You don't mean that."

"No," I admitted. "I don't mean it."

Levi got up from where he was sitting and came to sit next to me.

"I'm sorry. I know I screwed up. I should have waited before moving on. I know that now. I suppose I knew it at the time. I hurt you and I'm continuing to hurt you, and that's the last thing I want to do. But a woman is dead and I'm the prime suspect. Salinger is giving me a pass for now, but if the real killer isn't found…"

"You'll be a convenient scapegoat."

"Exactly. So will you help me?"

I closed my eyes and took a deep breath. "Okay, I'll help you."

"So maybe tomorrow…"

"I have a date tomorrow," I interrupted.

"A date?"

"Yes, a date. You do know what those are?"

"Yeah, it's just… never mind."

"I know George. If he's as mad at you as he was at Maddie I should be the one to talk to him. I'll find a time to work it in tomorrow. Perhaps you should chat up Beverly. And the sister; any idea where to find her?"

"I don't have a clue. The only reason I knew she was in town was because Maddie was complaining about it when I was at her place on the night she died."

"Do you have a last name?"

Levi shook his head.

"Do you have access to Maddie's classroom? Computer? Employee locker?"

"Yeah, I can get in."

"Okay, then look for info on the sister and anything else you can find. I'll keep my cell on during my date. Call me if you find anything."

"So who is this date with exactly?"

"Wouldn't you like to know."

Chapter 4

Saturday, February 13

I arrived at the Matthews household to find chaos. Hudson was running around the house in nothing but a diaper and one shoe and Haden had on a shirt that was wet on the front and shoes but no pants or diaper. Holly was sitting quietly on the couch with Mittens, but she was still in her pajamas. I could hear Brady upstairs cursing at something, although I wasn't sure what that something might be because all the kids were downstairs.

"Where's your dad?" I asked Holly.

"Upstairs. Haden took off his diaper and flushed it down the toilet. There's water all over the floor."

I picked up Haden and headed upstairs. I poked my head in the bathroom door to inform Brady that I would take charge of getting the kids dressed while he cleaned up what looked to be quite a large mess.

The poor guy looked exhausted. There was water down the front of him, it was apparent he hadn't had a chance to shower or shave, and there were bags under his eyes that hadn't been there the day before. Trying to be a single parent with three young children had to be nearly an impossible task. Up until a few days ago Brady had lived with his parents and had had their help. I was afraid he was in for a steep learning curve when it came down to figuring out how to do everything himself.

I changed Haden into a clean diaper, pants, and a shirt and then grabbed a set of clothes for Hudson and headed downstairs. Once I'd dressed him as well, I put them in their high chairs with a handful of Cheerios each, then instructed Holly to go get dressed. When she returned dressed in shorts and a tank top, I reminded her about the snow and told her to find long pants, a long-sleeved shirt, and a sweatshirt. Fortunately, she complied.

Meanwhile the cursing upstairs had stopped and had been replaced by banging as I imagined Brady was working on the pipes in an attempt to unclog the toilet. Maybe Zak should have hired Brady a live-in babysitter, like maybe a nanny. A very old and experienced grandmother type, not a young and beautiful nanny who marries her boss like in the romance novels I occasionally read.

The boys seemed fine strapped into their high chairs and Holly seemed happy playing with Mittens, so I decided to tackle the sink full of dirty dishes from breakfast. It looked like they'd had eggs and pancakes. At least it appeared Brady knew how to cook. I was just turning on the dishwasher when he poked his head into the kitchen.

"Thanks for seeing to the kids. I'm afraid we had a bit of a rough start this morning. The toilet is fixed, but I still need thirty minutes or so to take a shower and get ready. I hope that's not a problem."

"Not at all. The kids and I will hang out down here."

"I never realized how hard it was going to be to take care of everything on my own. Mom made it look easy."

"Your mom had practice being a mom. I'm sure things will be fine once you settle into a routine. Do you have a way to corral the boys when you aren't able to watch them? Maybe a playpen or a baby gate?"

"No, although now that you mention it, it would be helpful. I only turned my head for one minute. I'd dressed Haden and turned to look for clothes for Hudson and the next thing I knew Holly was running down the hall yelling about the water in the bathroom. Next time I'll put the clothed twin back into his crib while I dress his brother."

"That might be a good idea. Or at least close the bedroom door so they can't escape. Go ahead and take your shower. I'll add *buy playpen* to our list of activities today."

"You have a list?"

"Of course. I make a list for everything."

Brady smiled. I loved the way the corners of his eyes turned up, making him look like he was smiling with his whole face.

"Okay, then. I'll be back in a jiffy. I wouldn't want to mess up your carefully orchestrated plans."

I set both of the boys on the living room floor next to a pile of toys I'd found in a box next to the sofa. Then I sat down on the sofa to keep an eye on the destructive little buggers. Holly looked uncertain, but eventually she came over and sat down next to me.

"Are you going to be my new mommy?"

"No, honey. Why would you think that?"

"My grandma told my daddy that he needed to find us a new mommy. I thought it might be you."

"I'm just a friend. I work at the same place your daddy is going to work, so I'm helping him get settled."

"Do you have kids?"

"No. But I have a dog. His name is Shep. I'll introduce you sometime."

"Do you like kids?"

"I do. Very much."

Holly seemed satisfied with that answer because she returned her attention to Mittens, who had jumped up onto her lap. I could begin to see why Brady thought that living with his parents for the long term might be a mistake. It sounded like his mom was ready for him to move on, but that didn't mean he was.

It was snowing lightly by the time we made it into town. We decided to stop for lunch first because it was almost noon by the time we actually pulled onto Main Street. I hadn't eaten at Rosie's since my mom had sold it and moved in with her best friend, but the food was good, the atmosphere casual, and I knew there was a booth in the back that would be perfect for the five of us. I decided to set my mixed emotions over the transition to the side and suggested we eat there.

"I hope the food is as incredible as the view," Brady said after we walked into the reception area and he noticed the huge windows looking out onto the lake.

"It is. My mom used to own this place. She sold it recently, but the kitchen staff is the same." Or so I'd heard. Like I said, I hadn't actually been in myself. It felt so odd to enter the establishment as a guest when I'd grown up hanging out in the restaurant as the child of the owner.

"I was wondering when you would be in," the hostess greeted me.

"I've been meaning to stop by, but with my new job and all...This is Brady Matthews, the new math teacher at the Academy, and his children, Holly, Haden, and Hudson. Can we snag the big booth in the back?"

"Absolutely. I'll send your server right over."

I grabbed two high chairs and a booster seat for Holly. Once everyone was settled in I began to recite the menu by memory. Assuming they hadn't changed things much, I was confident I had a pretty good grip on where Mom had left things. All of the kids wanted grilled cheese and fruit, Brady decided on a prime rib sandwich, and I chose a turkey club. Once the server brought our beverages, I began to describe the layout of the town to Brady while we waited for our sandwiches.

"Almost all the retail establishments, with the exception of the new strip mall that will open soon on the highway leading out of town, are nestled within a three-block radius of Main Street, which parallels the lake. So, as you drive through town from east to west, the lake, the beach, and the landscaped park area is on your left and the row of shops and restaurants is on your right. Behind Main you'll find Second Street, and then Third, and so on. There's a residential neighborhood beginning on Fourth Street. The streets that intersect Main follow the alphabet, beginning with an A street on the west side of town."

"Sounds easy enough."

"It is. If you know your alphabet and can count to ten you can pretty much find your way around the town section of Ashton Falls. Of course there are a lot of homes that have been built outside the commercial area. I'll take you by the library, the schools, and the county offices. We'll be able to see pretty much everything in an hour or so."

"And the Academy?"

"We're housed in a temporary campus while the permanent one is being built. I'll show you where the temporary campus is. It'll be closed today because it's Saturday, but I'm sure Zak will give you a tour next week. After we're finished in town, I'd be happy to drive you out to the site where the permanent campus is being built."

"I'd like that."

"There's an awesome snow park just outside of town. I bet the kids would have fun sledding, and Holly is old enough to try ice skating. It would be fun to take them, although I'm not sure we'll have time today."

"Tomorrow? I'll even make you dinner when we get back."

I hesitated. Again, I had to ask if this was an offer of a date or if Brady was just being friendly. I decided it didn't really matter. An hour or two at the snow park followed by a cozy dinner with Brady and the kids sounded perfect.

"I'm babysitting two of the three kids Zak and Zoe have living with them. They're at Zoe's parents' house today, but I promised to pick them up tomorrow morning, along with Zoe's little sister, Harper, so Zoe's parents could have a quiet Valentine's Day."

"So bring them. The more the merrier."

"Okay." I smiled. "That sounds like a lot of fun."

The conversation paused as the waitress brought our food. It looked delicious.

"Tell me about the other teachers at the Academy," Brady suggested.

"Currently the students only attend classes at the Academy a half day, so we have a limited staff. Zak has plans to hire quite a few new staff members before the permanent campus opens in the fall. For the time being, he handles the computer science courses and has been filling in with the math since the other teacher left. The school principal, Phyllis King, teaches all the language arts courses, and the only other full-time staff member at this point is Ethan Carlton, who focuses on history and other social sciences. I think you're going to like everyone."

"I can't wait to meet them. The university I worked at last had hundreds of staff members. It was hard to get to know anyone who taught outside the math department."

Holly spilled her milk, ending the conversation. My dad would have had a fit and scolded me for not being careful if I did that when I was four, but Brady simply hugged Holly and assured her that accidents happened, while the waitress hurried into the kitchen for a towel to mop up the mess. Fortunately, Holly hadn't gotten her clothes wet, eliminating the need to go home and change her before we began our tour. I'd promised Levi I'd try to talk to George Wildwood today, so while Brady was buckling the kids into the car, I called his house and was told he was out at Eagle Lake ice fishing for the day. I decided I could keep my promise to Levi after I took Brady and the kids around town. Brady had mentioned the kids usually napped around two thirty, which would give me several hours to track George down before it got dark.

Eagle Lake was a large yet fairly shallow lake that froze solid enough each winter to provide a popular place to ice fish. I wasn't sure exactly where George would be, but his brother James, with whom he lived, had said he'd driven out to the lake in his big blue Dodge truck. My plan to find him consisted of driving slowly around the lake looking for the truck. Hopefully he hadn't quit for the day and was still there.

I'd dressed warmly for my walk around town with Brady and the kids, but the wind, coupled with the increased altitude where the lake was located, created at least a ten-degree drop in temperature compared to that in town. In other words, it was *cold*.

The lake was scattered with small wooden shacks where the fishermen hung out while they fished. Some were simply a stool positioned next to the ice hole, while others were more elaborate, with cushioned benches, ice chests, and even camp stoves.

It took about twenty minutes to find George's truck. He was on the side of the lake closest to the highway, a lucky break. I wasn't sure what the conditions of the lake road would be once it circled around to the back side.

I parked my own four-wheel drive next to George's truck, pulled my heavy down jacket over my wool sweater, and hurried toward the ice fishing hut. Hopefully it was warm inside.

"Ellie," George said when I entered through the small door. "What brings you out here on this cold day?"

"I guess you heard about Maddie."

"Yeah, I heard. Coffee?"

"No, thanks. I know you knew her; I was hoping you could give me some insight into what she was like."

"Isn't Zoe the resident sleuth in Ashton Falls?"

"She is, but she's away in Ireland. I wouldn't even bother looking into her death, but it affects a friend."

"Levi."

I noticed George's expression had grown guarded. "Yeah, Levi."

George adjusted the position of his pole, poured himself a cup of coffee, then sat back down. "Did Levi tell you Maddie and I had a good thing going until he came sniffing around?"

"He told me."

"I know the two of you were close at one point. Seems like you dodged a bullet, breaking things off with that one."

"Yeah, I guess. The sheriff thinks Maddie was drugged. Do you know who might want to hurt her?"

"Me for one. The woman used me. She let me think we were building something special together so I would pay off her debt. As soon as I did, she left me for your ex."

"Was it a lot of money?"

"Everything James and I had saved up for a new fishing boat. I felt like such a fool. Should have known a woman like her wouldn't really be interested in a man like me."

George had a point. In terms of datability, Maddie was eons out of George's league.

"You admit to having motive to kill Maddie. You didn't happen to act on that motive?" I wondered.

"No, I didn't. I was at Lucky's that night, shooting pool until closing. Lots of folks were there who can verify."

Lucky's closed at two a.m. and Salinger had said Maddie had died between ten and two, so I supposed it was possible he went straight from the bar to her place and killed her but not likely.

"Other than you, who had motive to kill her?"

George appeared to be considering my question. There'd been a huge part of me that thought he wouldn't even bother to talk to me. It wasn't like I had any official reason to be asking questions.

"If I had to pick a name I'd say Beverly Hallmark."

"Why Beverly?"

"She made it known to anyone who would listen that she had it bad for Levi. Beverly is a good-looking gal who isn't afraid to flaunt her assets. She's not used to being dumped and she definitely isn't used to being threatened."

"Threatened?"

"I was in the bar last week when Maddie came in looking for Levi. He wasn't there, but when Maddie saw Beverly she went right up to her and slapped her. She told her to stay away from her man and then she left. Whew-wee, was Bev ever mad. I'm not sure I've ever seen anyone turn quite that shade of red before."

"Wait, I thought Levi was with Bev before he hooked up with Maddie."

"He was. He dumped Bev and moved on to Maddie, but that didn't stop Bev from using every weapon in her arsenal to get Levi back. She wasn't sly about it either. She'd go right up to Levi and run her hand up his chest even if Maddie was standing right next to him."

I almost felt bad for Maddie. Almost.

"Okay, thanks for the information. Good luck with your fishing."

"Just about got my limit. Thinking of heading in for the night. You wouldn't want to get some dinner, would you?"

"Thank you for the offer, but I have a dinner date this evening. Enjoy your fish."

I decided to head back into town and then call Levi. The cell reception at the lake wasn't the best, and I wanted to be able to talk without the signal cutting in and out.

Levi and George had both mentioned Beverly as a suspect. Levi said he'd speak to Bev and I wondered if he had. As much as I resented Maddie for hooking up with Levi, I had to applaud her for slapping Bev. I should have done that when Levi and I were dating. Instead I'd endured a year of her flirting with Levi and putting me down.

The only other name on Levi's list was Maddie's sister, Lisa. I decided to call Salinger to ask if he'd contacted her. After all, she was the next of kin. Or at least one of them. I assumed both Maddie's parents were deceased if she was in charge of settling the estate. I didn't know if she had other siblings, but tracking down Lisa would be a good place to start.

I needed to stop off at the boathouse before heading over to Zak and Zoe's. When I pulled up I felt the same sense of homecoming I always did. Zoe actually still owned the boathouse. Her grandfather originally had built it to house his boat, but when the dam was destroyed and the lake level decreased, the building was useless for its original purpose. Zoe'd had the idea to convert it into a home and her grandfather had agreed. It sits right on the beach in one of the prettiest coves on the lake, a hop, skip, and jump down the beach from the big house where Zoe and Zak live.

The boathouse is small, with a living area, a kitchen, and a bath downstairs and a loft that's used as a bedroom upstairs. But what it lacks in size it makes up for in coziness. It has a rock fireplace that heats the entire building and a spectacular view of the lake. It's perfect for Shep and me, but if I do manage to make my dream of having a baby come true, I guess I'll have to move.

I gathered the things I needed from the boathouse and returned to Zoe's, where I let the dogs out while I called Salinger on my cell. He informed me that according to Maddie's employment records her next of kin was a cousin named Veronica. I thought it odd it wouldn't be her sister, so I decided to look into it further. Maddie's last name was Kramer; maybe Lisa's was as well. I took a chance and began calling nearby lodging properties. On my fourth try I hit pay dirt. Lisa Kramer was staying at the Ashton Falls Inn. Now all I had to do was convince her to talk to me.

I decided to call Levi first. I didn't want to waste my time talking to Lisa if he'd already located her and done so. He hadn't. We agreed we'd go to see her together, and he offered to pick me up.

Then he suggested we have dinner afterward. It seemed I'd spent more time with Levi in the past couple of days than I had when we were dating.

The Ashton Falls Inn was in the center of town. The desk clerk was happy to ring Lisa to ask her if she was willing to meet with us. She agreed to come down to the bar in ten minutes, so Levi and I headed there and ordered drinks.

I wasn't sure what I expected sexy, flirty Maddie's sister to be like, but it definitely wasn't the thin wallflower with a tendency to look at the floor while she spoke who greeted us.

"Thank you for agreeing to see us," I began. "I was sorry to hear about your sister."

Lisa looked down at her folded hands but didn't reply.

"I understand you came to town to speak to Maddie about an inheritance?" I asked.

"Yes. Mama was sick for a long time before she died. I stayed home and took care of her. It wasn't easy because she was a very demanding woman, but she needed the help and I loved her." Lisa took a deep breath before she continued. "After she passed I found out Mama had left me and Maddie the house equally. I assumed that because I'd been living there the past five years taking care of Mama, I'd be allowed to stay, but Maddie said it would be best if we sold the house. I didn't want to sell. The house is my home and I don't have anywhere else to go. I tried to talk to Maddie about it, but she wouldn't listen, so I came here to talk to her face-to-face."

"And now that she's dead…?"

Lisa shrugged. "I guess the house is mine. I still need to talk to the lawyer to know for certain, but we have no other siblings."

"Do you know why Maddie wanted to sell?" I couldn't help but think that as her sister, Maddie should have wanted to see Lisa taken care of. She had, after all, sacrificed five years of her life taking care of their mother.

"I guess she wanted the money. Maddie thought I'd been taking advantage of Mama because I lived with her for so long, but it wasn't like that. She just didn't understand how sick Mama really was."

"Didn't she ever visit?"

"No. Maddie and Mama didn't get along."

I looked at Levi. He shrugged. We'd agreed that I would handle the interview unless it looked like Lisa was the type to be charmed by his wicked smile. It didn't seem she was.

"Did you have a chance to speak to Maddie?"

"No. She was supposed to come meet me for dinner on Wednesday night, but she never showed up. I guess she had something better to do."

Like hang out with my ex-boyfriend.

"If there's anything I can do to help you while you're in town please let me know," I offered.

Lisa smiled.

Levi and I said good-bye and headed to the car.

"Why didn't you ask about an alibi?" Levi asked after we pulled onto the highway leading toward the restaurant where Levi wanted to eat.

"There's no way that sweet thing killed her sister," I answered.

"She didn't seem the type, but she did have a motive and you can't always tell a book by its cover."

"In this case I think we can assume she's exactly who she appears to be. Did you talk to Beverly?"

He nodded.

"And...?"

"And she said she worked until closing the night Maddie died. I suppose that would be easy enough to verify."

I frowned. Something didn't feel right. If George's alibi was that he was at the bar until closing and Beverly worked until then, he would have known she was there, yet he'd suggested she was a suspect. One of them was lying.

Chapter 5

Dinner with Levi was perfect. It made me remember why I'd thought we'd be good together. We laughed and talked about old times just like we used to. I suppose if not for the issue between us regarding children, we might have ended up marrying. Although if I were being honest, having children wasn't our only source of conflict. It seemed we just weren't as committed to each other as two people who planned to spend their lives together should have been.

"It's early yet," I said after we'd finished eating. "What do you say we stop by Lucky's to talk to the bartender? It seems either George or Beverly is lying about being there until closing. Or, if they both were there, George intentionally misled me, which makes me wonder why."

"I could go for a drink. Just let me pay the check."

I handed Levi some money. "I'll pay for my half."

He looked like he was going to argue, but then he accepted the money and flagged down the waitress.

Lucky's was a seedy bar where beer and whiskey were the drinks of choice and everyone ignored the law despite the fact that there were No Smoking signs posted everywhere. It wasn't at all my type of place, but I'd accompanied Levi there on several occasions because he enjoyed playing pool with the men and women who frequented the establishment. I suppose visiting Lucky's was one of the little things I'd done to show Levi just how much I loved him, though now I wondered what sacrifices Levi had ever made for me.

"Two drafts," Levi ordered when we walked up to the bar and sat down. There was a new bartender tonight who I'd never met before. Not that I came in all that often. The old guy who was usually behind the bar gave me the creeps, but this one was downright scary. Not only was he tall and burly but he had a tattoo of a snake eating a rat on his neck. Talk about intimidating. I didn't see Beverly; maybe she was off that night.

"Are you new in town?" Levi asked conversationally.

"Been here a few months."

"Mind answering a few questions?"

"Got any money?"

Levi slipped the bartender a twenty. "I need to know if Bev worked last Wednesday."

The bartender took the money. "She did."

"And George Wildwood...was he here as well?"

"Yeah, he was here. Came in with his brother."

"Did he stay until closing?"

The bartender held out his hand. Levi handed him another twenty.

"I'm not sure," he replied after he pocketed the cash. "I left early. It was slow, so one of the servers covered for me, but George was here when I left at around one. James left earlier in the evening, though. Say around eleven. I remember it was right around the time Bev took her break. I have a feeling the two of them might have hooked up. Bev came back looking disheveled."

"Bev took a break?" I asked. "How long was she gone?"

"She has a half hour, but now that I think about it, it did seem like she was gone a long time. Why do you want to know?"

I just looked at Levi, who shrugged.

"Have you seen Bev and James together before?" I asked.

The bartender drummed his fingers on the bar as if to remind me that I had to pay for information.

"Nope," he answered once Levi had slipped him yet another twenty. This was getting ridiculous.

I looked at the bartender. "That's it? Twenty bucks only buys us a 'nope'?"

"Ask a question, get an answer."

"Does Bev often hook up with patrons during her breaks?"

He just looked at me.

"Seriously? You want more money?"

The bartender smiled, showing off his crooked yellow teeth.

Levi opened his wallet to show me that it was empty. I pulled a ten-dollar bill out of my pocket. "This is all I have, but before I give it to you I want you to answer a two-part question."

"Okay, shoot."

"Did James come back to the bar after Bev's break and have you seen them together since?"

"Nope and nope."

"Okay; thank you." I slid the ten-dollar bill across the sticky bar to the man. "Let's get out of here," I said to Levi.

Levi followed me out to his truck. I slid inside and then turned to look at him. "I have a new theory," I began. "George said the money Maddie took from him was everything he and James had saved up to buy a new boat. What if James is the killer? Or at least one of them? It almost sounds like James and Bev could be in on it together. They both had motive to want to get back at Maddie."

"Makes sense. But how do we prove it?"

"I'm not sure," I admitted. "Maybe we can play one of them against the other."

"And how exactly do we do that?"

"Let's go back to the house. I need to let the dogs out. We can have a glass of wine and come up with a plan. You know, this is kinda fun. I guess I can see how Zoe lets herself get pulled into these investigations."

"Yeah, but Zoe has almost died a bunch of times. Let's not do that."

"Agreed."

There were snow flurries in the air as we drove back to Zak and Zoe's. It was nice to sit with Levi in companionable silence. Things had been weird between us since we'd split. Now we were both trying for a sense of normalcy, but it seemed it had been a long time in coming. I hoped that when Zoe got back from her trip we could all start hanging out like we used to before Levi and I had become exes.

"You know," I said as he pulled into the circular drive off the private road that led to the Zimmerman house, "Salinger never said anything about there being any sign of a struggle. It almost makes me think James really is the killer. Would it have made sense for Maddie to just invite Bev inside if the two of them didn't get along?"

"Good point," Levi said as we both unbuckled our seat belts. "So how do we prove it?"

"Maybe we should just call Salinger and fill him in. We did both agree not to walk blindly into potentially dangerous situations."

"I doubt James poses much of a threat. The guy is shorter than you are. I'm pretty sure that if push came to shove I could take him."

"I'm sure you could, but just because he's slight doesn't mean he doesn't have a gun."

"Okay, how about this," Levi began as we opened the back door and let the dogs out into the yard. "Why don't we pretend we simply want to chat with him about Bev? We won't let on that we consider him to be a suspect. Maybe we can get him to tell us what we really want to know without him even knowing we're there to interrogate him."

The dogs returned to the house and Levi and I worked together to get everyone fed. In addition to the four dogs, there were three cats who had been hanging around upstairs. It was a good thing Zoe had a large house because she had a tendency to collect animals.

"Okay," I agreed after I'd had a chance to think about Levi's suggestion for a few minutes. "But let's meet him in a public place, not at his house." I looked at the clock. It had been dark for a while, but it was only eight thirty. "Maybe we can offer to buy him some pie at the diner near where he lives. I'll call him. We've chatted in the past and he was a regular at both Rosie's and the Beach Hut. He seemed to like me."

"Okay, call him. If he'll meet us in the diner that seems like a pretty safe way to interview him. If we still think he's a suspect after we talk to him, we'll call Salinger."

"Fine."

George and James lived outside of town, just off the highway that led down the mountain. The diner nearest their home was famous for its pies, although I didn't think they were nearly as good as the ones my mom made. I used all the charm I could muster to convince James that I really could use his help with my investigation and would be so grateful if he'd agree to speak to me. Levi and I had agreed that I would get more out of James if I spoke to him alone, so Levi reluctantly complied with my suggestion that he wait in the car.

"Thank you for speaking to me," I said to James as I slipped into the booth across from him.

"I'm happy to help, but I'm still not sure why you're running around asking questions about Maddie Kramer's murder. George told me that you spoke to him as well."

"I'm just trying to help out while Zoe's out of town. The bartender at Lucky's mentioned you were in there the night Maddie died, so I hoped you might be able to answer a few questions about Bev."

James motioned for the waitress to refresh his coffee. "Pie?" he asked.

"Sure. I'll take a small slice of the banana cream." I didn't really want any, but pie was the excuse I'd used to get James to meet me. He ordered a piece of blueberry with ice cream and we resumed our conversation.

"Okay," James said after the waitress left to get our pie. "What do you want to know?"

"What time did you get to Lucky's last Wednesday?"

"Guess around eight, give or take thirty minutes."

"And did you go alone?"

"No. George was with me. There was nothing on the tube, so we decided to shoot some pool."

I smiled at the tired-looking waitress as she set our plates in front of us. I'd waited enough tables during my life to know how tired you can be at the end of your shift.

"And Bev was working that night?" I confirmed.

"Yeah, she was there. This pie is good. How's yours?"

I took a small bite. "Delicious."

It wasn't.

"Do you remember if Bev was there the entire time you were?"

"Yeah, she was there. Had on a skirt so short you couldn't help but notice."

I took a sip of my coffee. "Do you remember what time you left the bar?"

James took another bite of his pie, slowly chewed, and then swallowed before he answered. "I'm guessing around eleven. George didn't want to leave, but I was tired. We came together, so I couldn't really head home until he did, but Bev said she had a break and offered to drive me home."

Which explained, I realized, why they'd left together.

"That was nice of her. Sounds like she might be sweet on you."

James blushed. "Naw. I wouldn't mind spending some time with her, but I'm pretty sure she has another guy. When I asked her to come in she said she had to meet someone."

"She didn't say who?"

"No, but I could tell by the look in her eye that she was heading out to get herself some carnal delight."

Carnal delight?

"That woman sure does seem to enjoy her share of male companionship," James added.

Yes, she certainly did.

"Do you remember when George got home?" I asked.

"No. Like I said, I was tired and went to bed. Look, I know you said you wanted to help out, but that woman broke George's heart. I'm not sure she was worth the effort you're putting into this."

"Maybe you're right. I do appreciate your taking the time to talk to me."

"Happy to. I miss our chats now that the Hut is closed."

I put my hand over James's and gave it a squeeze. "I miss them too. This has been nice, and you may be right about Maddie not being worth my time. I was sorry to hear about your losing the money you'd saved for a new boat."

"Sorry? What do you mean, sorry?"

"I'm afraid I blew it," I said to Levi after I returned to the truck. "George hadn't told James about the money he gave to Maddie. He had no idea it was gone."

"He was going to find out eventually."

"I know. But I feel bad that I let the cat out of the bag. James wasn't happy. I'm sure George is going to get an earful when he gets home. It does prove that James probably didn't kill Maddie, though. If he didn't know about the money it eliminates his motive."

"So we're back to Bev?"

"Maybe." I told Levi what I'd found out about Bev giving James a ride home on the night of the murder, and that she'd indicated that she was meeting someone. "James seemed to think she was heading toward a hookup of the male/female variety, but was she?"

"So what now?" Levi wondered.

"I don't know. I'm tired and it's getting late. I say we sleep on it and see if something comes to us."

"Do you want to meet up tomorrow?" Levi inquired.

"I'm taking Alex, Scooter, and Harper to the snow park. If I think of anything I'll call you."

"Do you want me to come to the snow park with you?"

"Actually, we're going with Brady Matthews and his family. We'll be going to his place for dinner afterward, so I really won't be free all day. Like I said, I'll call you if I think of anything."

I leaned over to kiss Levi on the cheek when he pulled up in front of Zoe's. I couldn't help noticing he looked like a sad little boy who hadn't been invited to the party. "I'd ask you to come with us, but I think it's best if the two of us solidify our status as friends before we bring potential love interests into the picture."

"Is this Brady Matthews a 'potential love interest'?"

I smiled. "Honestly, it's too soon to tell."

Chapter 6

Sunday, February 14

Holly bonded with Alex the moment I introduced them and Alex seemed equally enchanted with Holly. Scooter had asked to bring his friend Tucker along to the snow park, which was a good thing; Holly attached herself to Alex so firmly it was obvious she had no intention of sharing her with Scooter or anyone else. Even Haden and Hudson seemed to be having a wonderful time helping their dad build the most pathetic snowman I had ever seen. I couldn't remember when I'd had such a wonderful time.

The fresh snow we'd had the past week slowed down the hills to the point that we felt it was safe for Holly to sled down with Alex. Of course once the twins saw how much fun their sister was having, they wanted to try it too, so Brady and I each took one of the boys down the tiniest hill we could find. The ride was both slow and short, but the twins screamed with delight and begged to do it over and over again.

After an hour the boys let us know they were tired and Brady took them back to the car for a diaper change and a bottle while I watched the older kids make their final runs. It made my heart happy to see them having so much fun. I found myself praying the doctor was right and they'd develop a procedure to help me conceive before I was too old to safely do so. The thought of missing the chance to experience fun family events with my own children filled me with a longing that reached clear down to my soul.

"Who's the little girl with Alex?" Sarena Pewter, a waitress from Rosie's who I'd known for years, commented as she walked over to where I was standing.

"Her name is Holly Matthews. She's the daughter of the new math teacher at Zimmerman Academy."

"I was sorry to hear Will left town. He was a good customer and a good tipper."

Will Danner, the teacher Brady had been hired to replace, had moved east to be closer to his elderly father shortly after the new year.

"Yeah, everyone really misses him, but I think Brady is going to fit right in. Are you here with your family?"

"They wanted to hike up and do the big hill and I didn't have the energy so I told them I'd wait here. I hoped Levi was with you. I wanted to talk to him about a football camp he's mentioned. My second son wants to try out for the football team next year and he could use some pointers."

"Levi and I broke up a couple of months ago."

"I kind of assumed that when I noticed him coming and going from Maddie's place, but when I noticed that his visits seemed to stop and a new guy started coming and going in his place, I thought maybe you'd gotten back together."

I'd forgotten that Sarena lived two doors down from Maddie; anyone who came and went from Maddie's place would have to pass by her front window. "A new guy?"

Sarena shrugged. "I don't know his name, but it seemed like he'd become a frequent visitor."

"Can you tell me what he looked like?"

"Big guy, husky, long dark hair. He didn't seem like her type, but he'd been coming around pretty often so I just made the leap and assumed they were together."

"Do you remember when you saw him last?"

Sarena thought about it. "I guess it was Wednesday. Late. After midnight. I had an early morning the next day and I couldn't sleep, so I got up to heat up some milk."

"The night Maddie died."

"Maddie's dead?" Sarena gasped.

"I figured you must have heard."

"We went away early on Thursday to attend the funeral of my husband's aunt. We just got back today. No one has mentioned it to me, but then, I really haven't talked to anyone. I can't believe she's dead. What happened?"

"Someone put sleeping pills in her wine. At least that's what the sheriff thinks happened. I suppose technically he can't rule out the possibility that she put the drug in her own drink, but it makes no sense that she'd grind them up. Salinger is going to need to find out who this guy was. Can you think of anything specific about him?"

Sarena thought about it. "He had a tattoo on his neck."

Suddenly I knew exactly who'd killed Maddie. I excused myself from Sarena so I could call Salinger. Zoe would have confronted the guy on her own, but I'm not the supersleuth type. I've always been the much less brave and more cautious sidekick. As far as I was concerned, I'd done my job; it was time to turn things over to the pro.

"You really are a wonderful cook," I said to Brady later that evening.

"You sound surprised."

"I guess I am. I'm sorry for doubting you when you told me that you were. I shouldn't be so surprised. Zak is an excellent cook and it seems like the two of you are a lot alike."

"I'll take that as a compliment."

"You should. Zak is a great guy. What did you put in the sauce? It has such a unique flavor."

"It's my secret, but if you want to come to dinner again later in the week I might be willing to share my recipes with you."

"Deal. This is delicious. Really. The best pasta I've ever had."

"Trish didn't really like to cook, so I helped out whenever I could. The more time I spent in the kitchen the more I found that cooking was relaxing after so much mental activity. It gave me a sense of comfort to go through familiar motions at the end of the day. I began experimenting and creating my own recipes and fell in love with the craft. Don't get me wrong—I love math and I enjoy teaching—but if I had to choose a second career, I'd most definitely want to be a chef. For me cooking is both primal and sensual. It fills a part of my soul that can't be touched in any other way."

I felt my heart pounding as Brady talked about his love of the activity we both enjoyed. "I know exactly what you mean. When I'm creating a new recipe it's like I'm totally lost in a different world. It's just me, the food, and the kitchen."

"I know you owned your own sandwich shop, but did you ever consider going to culinary school?"

"I suppose it went through my mind from time to time, but school is expensive, and I knew my mom couldn't really manage it. I worked at her restaurant from the time I was a teen. It was easy to just continue to do it when I graduated high school."

"There was never a doubt in my mind I would go to college. It was expected in our family. In fact, I remember one time—"

My phone rang, interrupting Brady. I looked at the caller ID. "I'm sorry, I need to take this. I'll just be a minute." I walked into the living room, where I could have some privacy.

"So, was I right?" I asked Salinger when I answered his call.

"I have the feeling you might be. The guy isn't admitting to anything at the moment, but I did manage to find out that he moved to Ashton Falls recently."

"Yeah, he mentioned he'd only been here for a few months."

"Interestingly enough, he moved to the area from the same small town Maddie lived in before she arrived in town eighteen months ago. So far I haven't been able to prove they knew each other, but it seems likely. I'm working on it. In the meantime, I'd like to speak to your friend: the one who told you that she'd seen a guy pass by her window. I'll need an eyewitness to continue to hold the guy while I get this sorted out."

I gave Salinger Sarena's phone number before hanging up and returning to the kitchen.

"Everything okay?" Brady asked.

"Yeah. It was Sheriff Salinger. He picked up the bartender at Lucky's. It looks like my hunch about Maddie Kramer's murderer is going to pay off."

"I'm glad things worked out. I have to admit that one of the reasons I decided to take the job at Zimmerman Academy was because of Ashton Falls' low crime rate. What are the odds there would be a murder investigation going on my first week here?"

I wondered if I should tell him that we had more murders per capita than pretty much any other small town in the country, but why scare the guy away? I just smiled and hoped the murder trend we'd been having would end as abruptly as it had begun.

"You know, I was really dreading today, but I've had one of the best days I've had in a long time," Brady commented. "It's hard to be alone and missing the person you love any day of the year, but it's especially bad on special days like holidays and birthdays."

"Did you have a Valentine's Day tradition with your wife?"

"We did. Every year since we were married we spent Valentine's Day at this little bed-and-breakfast we discovered shortly after we started dating."

"That sounds nice."

"It was." A look of sadness came over Brady's face. "How about you? Any Valentine's traditions?"

"No. I'm afraid I've never been with any one person long enough to establish a tradition. I really love the idea of having one, though. Something you can look forward to year after year."

"It'll happen. You'll find that special guy."

"I hope so."

Brady hung the dish rag over the edge of the sink. He turned around and leaned against the counter. He crossed his arms over his chest before he began to speak. "As I was boarding the plane to come to Ashton Falls, I had a moment of doubt that I was doing the right thing. I thought I wanted to move on and start fresh somewhere else, which was why I applied for the job at the Academy, but in that final moment I began to wonder if leaving everything behind that was predictable and normal was really the right thing to do. In the past few days, after getting to know you and meeting some of the people in town, I feel certain I made the right decision. I find that I'm actually excited getting up in the morning and finding out what my new life is going to look like. The fact of the matter is, Ellie Davis, you've been good for me."

I smiled.

"I hope we can continue to spend time together once the weekend is over and the normal routine of your week resumes," he added.

"I'd like that. You've been good for me too. The day I picked you up at the airport was shaping up to be one of the worst ones of my life, but then we talked about finding a new normal when the old normal has ceased to exist, and I realized I needed to let go of what I'd lost and start building something new. Our talk helped me more than you'll ever know."

Brady filled two bottles with milk. "Do you want to help me get the boys tucked in?"

"I'd love to."

He handed one of the bottles to me. He held it up and clicked it against mine, as if in a toast. "To us and our friendship, and to finding a wonderful and fulfilling *new normal* in the year ahead."

Kathi Daley lives with her husband, kids, grandkids, and Bernese mountain dogs in beautiful Lake Tahoe. When she isn't writing, she likes to read (preferably at the beach or by the fire), cook (preferably something with chocolate or cheese), and garden (planting and planning, not weeding). She also enjoys spending time on the water when she's not hiking, biking, or snowshoeing the miles of desolate trails surrounding her home.

Kathi uses the mountain setting in which she lives, along with the animals (wild and domestic) that share her home, as inspiration for her cozy mysteries.

Stay up-to-date with her newsletter, *The Daley Weekly*. There's a link to sign up on both her Facebook page and her website, or you can access the sign-in sheet at: http://eepurl.com/NRPDf

Visit Kathi:

Facebook at Kathi Daley Books, www.facebook.com/kathidaleybooks

Kathi Daley Books Group Page – https://www.facebook.com/groups/569578823146850/

Webpage - www.kathidaley.com

E-mail - kathidaley@kathidaley.com

Made in the USA
Charleston, SC
06 January 2016